# MIND
# WANDERER

BY

EVAN A. CUSHING

# CONTENTS

PROLOGUE:
AND SO I BEGIN AGAIN... .........................1

CHAPTER ONE:
ONE LIFE FOR ANOTHER........................5

CHAPTER TWO:
THE END OF NORMAL ...........................13

CHAPTER THREE:
BLOOD DRIVE.........................................21

CHAPTER FOUR:
SHARDS OF PEACE................................29

CHAPTER FIVE:
BURNING DESIRE ..................................39

CHAPTER SIX:
FROZEN HOPE.  COOL RESOLVE. .....47

CHAPTER SEVEN:
THE END OF NORMAL DAYS...............53

# PROLOGUE:
# AND SO I BEGIN AGAIN...

In a battle that had raged for thousands of years, a man, whose first memories came from life in now ancient Rome as a military commander, fought a woman, his rival, once a prophetess of the Celts. The battleground: a dark hill outside a sleepy little town, a thunderstorm raging around them as they raged at each other. Fiery blade met lightning-sheathed staff. Both combatants bled. Both were burned. After thousands of years, inhabiting hundreds of different bodies, they still were evenly matched. The only things that were truly their own always were the skills and powers they had and their memories and mindsets that had traveled from form to form for ages almost uncounted.

The tall, heavily muscled, fair-skinned, blond-haired, brown-eyed man, with a huge flaming axe, who wielded fire and earth as if soft clay, and had once upon a time commanded armies, bent the earth to his will trying to quench the life of his eternal foe. With a roar he bellowed, "This ends now, witch! I never asked for this!"

The tall, pale-skinned, black-haired, green-eyed female in front of him scowled and murmured, "I keep telling this meathead I am not to blame," as she jumped out of the way of a giant fist shaped from the wet soft ground beneath her feet, trying to grab her. She summoned lightning as if from thin air and struck at the man in front of her.

"Damn you Graya, the curse will not end like this. I will not end like this!" the man howled, as he tried to block the bolt with his axe held over his head, legs braced against the rain-slick mud pile on which they fought, as they had thousands and thousands of times before.

"I know that, Corewayin. This cycle will just go on as always. I am frankly very tired of dying only to repeat this in a new form," as she pressed the bolt of electricity further through his guard toward his heart. How had it come to this, she wondered. She had once loved this man thousands of years before. But the gift of eternal uninhibited life the both of them, among a few others throughout earth's history, possessed, was far more a curse, just as her former lover had said so many times before. Just living for so long through so many lives did something to them, to anyone knowingly reborn in other bodies so many times.

The hugely muscled man called Corewayin, his first name but not his last, grunted under the force of power he was holding back as he was thrown onto his back, burned and dying again.

Graya, also the woman's first name, but once used more like a title, was the name always given to the firstborn daughter of each generation of god speakers, the family of high priests and priestesses of her tribe, a tribe that had long since died out after the Roman army took over her tribe's lands and slew them almost to a soul. Corewayin was the man who had saved her life and those of a few other women and children the day her tribe's last camp burned around them.

And as the winner of their fights had always done before, she now rushed over to him to hear any regrets he had, or an apology — anything to make their rage and hate seem even a bit misplaced.

This time he died slowly, burned and broken, and as he coughed up some blood he spoke matter-of-factly, as if spewing up blood and looking like a badly done pig roast was totally normal, which in his case it almost was. He said as she held him, "Well, you are still getting better."

She was trying and failing to not look sad, as she spoke in an almost firm voice, "Yes, but eight hundred years ago, if I had done something like that you would have been dead in an instant, although we both had far more true magic back then."

Corewayin said sadly with a pained grimace due more to his wounds than his feelings, "Kind of funny that true magic is a dead art form for everyone but those like us."

Graya nodded and said sadly, "But the monsters that follow us are real enough."

Corewayin grinned and said, "The last time you were like this was two hundred years ago. After I woke up in that old stone coffin in Scotland, you and your human minions at the time battled me to the death, all the way to Moscow where you held me just like this."

Graya smiled and said, "But we were both coughing up blood then."

Corewayin grinned and said, "Next time we meet I'd like to hunt the monsters that track me down before we duke it out. Well, see ya." Then Corewayin's body went limp in Graya's arms. They had both died so many times that they were experts at knowing the exact second when their current body would die.

Graya sighed as she herself felt her life waning. "Sooner than you think, you meathead," as she sat on the muddy ground, on that lonely hill, near a small town, as the thunderstorm was ebbing, dying. She had used up far too much of her power and now her wounds and fatigue, along with the strain of all the magic she had used, were dragging her down unto death, again.

# CHAPTER ONE:
# ONE LIFE FOR ANOTHER

*First day back among the living for the damned*, the boy thought as he opened his eyes. A young fair-skinned, brown-haired teenage girl was sitting next to the hospital bed he found himself in. She was asleep in a chair, head down, lightly drooling on a light cream-colored shirt, hands on her pink skirt, light brown boots on her limp feet. "And so it begins again," he grumbled.

At his words, she woke up with a start and almost shouted, "Oh Jonathan, you're up! Um, how are you brother? How do you feel?"

Corewayin's mind was now in his new body, the mind of the boy Jonathan all but obliterated save for a few memories. The body that this Jonathan had occupied once had a twin sister; the last memory was something hazy about a big storm.

Corewayin chose to play it safe. He kind of wanted to experience the life of a normal child, for a time, at least. "What happened, Sarah?" he asked, remembering his new body's twin's name.

Her bright green eyes stared at him for a few seconds with something that seemed like relief and said, "Hold on, let me get Mom and Dad. They will be thrilled to see you are ok, and they can tell you better than I can." Corewayin, now Jonathan, could tell his new twin sister was trying very hard to hold back tears, and that she was unsure what was safe to tell him. Only the many, many centuries of dealing with others made reading folks so simple and reflexive for him.

As the girl rushed out of the room, Corewayin started to sift through the memories of the body he now inhabited. The boy Jonathan had been in an accident of some kind, but a disturbing number of memories the boy had were jumbled and hazy. "Good," Corewayin mumbled from this new body, he had a ready-made excuse for acting unlike the previous resident of his new body, and it seemed like he had taken over the body of someone that was in great pain and distress, so unlike most of the other existences he had cut short due to his own deaths. This one was rather guilt free, because too swiftly leaving his new family would be problematic in many ways.

After a time, a middle-aged man and woman rushed in, the girl Sarah right behind them and a doctor at their heels. Before any of them could say anything, Corewayin, now acting in his role of Jonathan, smiled and said, "Hey Mom, Dad, sis, doc — so how bad is it? I can head back to school soon, I hope."

The four mortals in his hospital room's doorway stopped in their tracks, mouths agape. The doctor seemed to be most in shock, while Jonathan's twin sister seemed to be almost half expecting something of the sort, though clearly none of them were fully ready for such a coherent statement from his hospitalized form.

The middle-aged woman that, from Jonathan's memories, Corewayin recognized as the mother of his current body, was named Wendy Hope. The women asked, "What's the last thing you recall? How do you feel?"

She would have asked more if not for the slightly overweight male doctor in the back of the room, who put his hand on her shoulder and said, "You can ask your questions later. I have some tests to run, and would prefer not to burden the patient with too many details just yet."

The other man in the room, Jonathan's father, Corewayin recalled, whose name was Jeff Hope, nodded and said, "Ok doctor, we will wait outside. Please let us know how he is. We would like to visit him again soon." Then to Corewayin he said, "Ok champ, we will be nearby."

Sarah, on the verge of tears, added as the family of the boy Jonathan filed out of the room, "Get well soon, brother."

As the door closed behind them, the doctor looked at Corewayin strangely and said, "Odd form you got there this time, form jumper."

Corewayin nodded and said, "Let me guess. Swamp troll. Elder breed?"

The doctor smiled, letting a few bits of his illusionary form slip. The inhumanly wide shark-like jaw, the few scaly pockmarks shown through the facade, the malevolent wisdom in the reptilian eyes all told Corewayin he was absolutely correct.

"So what now?" asked Corewayin as politely as he could. Ticking off a troll this powerful before his current form was fully recovered, in a hospital no less, was pure suicide.

The troll resumed his guise of a dumpy unassuming doctor slightly on in years, very fitting for a man-eating swamp troll of the elder line in a rather ironically fitting way, but one that was likely very fulfilling for the beast. The troll said, "I'll let you go after some rehab work that you likely do not truly need, but try to act like you do. Then my debt will be repaid. You are not to show that you know what I really am, or else."

Corewayin grinned and said, "Been a while, Thrak. Ok, yeah, deal, and thanks for that."

Thrak the troll's doctor guise grimaced and said, "It's unnerving how perceptive you are, but I exist only because of the power you bled off while fighting that fire giant. But really, a fire giant, how did a troll like myself come into being in front of that?" The doctor shivered then added, "Anyway, I'll let your stolen form's new family know you are ok. Just stay with them for a bit, at least. They are truly very nice, and you need a vacation from the war."

Corewayin smiled with Jonathan's face and said, "Thanks for that, and yeah totally, even now, no questions asked."

And so, after two weeks, even due to his powers of healing and fitness-enhancing properties, the physical rehab was still a bit of a struggle, but far more simple than any of the mortals were expecting. In fact, he was putting on lots of muscle, and that was likely why he was released, the staff at the hospital almost panicking at the speed of his recovery. Apparently his new body had been on his new family's roof in a rainstorm and fell face first onto a gravel sidewalk around a month before. Everyone was expecting at best serious brain damage, but a week before he woke up, which was the day after his last body had died, stronger life signs were suddenly detected in his current body. Given the haziness of many of the memories belonging to the boy Jonathan, Corewayin could tell that if he had not taken control, the body would not have lived a full complete life, if at all, so at least he did not have many regrets about that this time around.

As Corewayin was being discharged from the hospital into the care of his current body's still oblivious family, Thrak was there to see him off. Thrak's alias was Murphy Grillen. Apparently he was one of three surgeons in the small hospital's intensive care unit, and the oldest one at that, although just how old, the mortals around him no doubt had no idea.   Thrak was accidentally brought into existence by Corewayin from residual true magic a little over five hundred years before in a fight against a third generation fire giant.  Elder breeds were the first of the monsters, but they could make weaker versions of themselves in a similar way to a form jumper like Corewayin.

The best way to for form jumpers and monsters to regain magic was by killing those that had it and absorbing it, for the earth had been steadily drained of most of its naturally occurring magic.  Elder breeds had more magic than the other monsters, as they were more powerful, and so the best way for a form jumper to gain power fast was to hunt them.  But as form jumpers would just inhabit a new body when killed and monsters could not, monsters and form jumpers realty hated one another, for the most part.

For some reason, the elder breeds Corewayin created (unconsciously, for the most part, as summoning monsters on purpose was often very risky) were a bit more cunning and mellow then those made by other form jumpers. Most of Corewayin's creations were, while not friendly with him, not out for blood either (although the man-eating ones did enjoy gore when it would not be tracked to them).

And so as Corewayin left the hospital as the young high school boy Jonathan Hope, doctor Murphy Grillen stopped the extremely relieved family and said to them, "Now I just want to be sure you all understand this. Jonathan was extremely lucky this time. It is astounding to the staff here that he is able to walk, let alone think clearly, but do not be surprised if he has some trouble remembering the past few months."

After that, Thrak, still in the guise of Murphy, addressed Corewayin directly, saying "Now young man, you may be able to run, but do not push yourself." The meaning behind this was *do not show off in front of the mortals.*

Corewayin, as Jonathan, grinned and said, "No worries. I know my limits, doc. I swear I'll be careful and not trouble you again," meaning *yeah, I know, thanks, and do not worry; your secret is safe with me, Thrak.*

The doctor smiled and said, "Ok, that's what I like to hear," then to Sarah Hope, he added, "Look after your brother, sweetie."

She just looked away and said in a mildly pouty tone, "Yeah, fine."

After that, the Hope family, Corewayin's body included, got in the family's four-seater car.

On the way back to their home, with Jeff Hope driving to the quite out-of-the-way neighborhood the Hope family lived in, Wendy Hope asked, "Sarah, how is that friend of yours doing? I hope she is ok."

Corewayin asked, "So, um, what happened?" Then to Sarah's quizzical and concerned face he elaborated in Jonathan's voice, "What? I've been out cold for like forever. Any news would help to center myself a bit, plus sis, if you are worried about someone, the least I can do is hear you out."

Jeff, still driving, laughed as he said "Son, you are so mature now."

Sarah was staring. It seemed like they were expecting a trouble-making teenage boy, not a three thousand year old mind in a teenage boy's body, not that Corewayin, as Jonathan, would correct them on that. Wendy spoke up and said "I know dear, not too long ago they would be pulling each other's hair by now."

Still staring at Corewayin, Sarah said in a mildly bewildered tone, "About a week ago, at my late night dance class, Beth Summers fell down a long flight of stairs, but she is fine now. I think she is still a bit shook up."

"Oh," Corewayin said, "Well if you need any help, you can ask me."

Sarah stared at her twin's face even more as she said to Corewayin, "Jon, you two have always hated each other, but if I think you can help, I'll ask." The tone in her voice said how very unlikely that seemed to Sarah, but Corewayin was interested because it was possible Graya his old rival had taken over the mind of Beth Summers, his current body's twin's friend.

They arrived at the Hope family home, brown and two-floored, a bit cramped with two teenage children (although one of those now was a lot older mentally then he had been). They pulled up and walked through the fount door into the home's hallway and put their shoes away. Corewayin looked at a very old photo of a woman that seemed familiar. He recalled from the memories of Jonathan Hope that she was some distant relative that his body's original owner had never really paid any mind to. He inquired, "Hey, remind me who this photo is of." Wendy Hope looked over and said, "Oh that's Beatrice Hope, a distant ancestor of mine from around 200 years ago." Corewayin looked closely at the old photo of a woman standing with a small child, but no one else; then he changed the subject. "So do I go to school tomorrow? I feel up for it."

Jeff Hope smiled and answered, "Well yeah, but if you feel ill or anything, go to the nurse's office and we will pick you up. I'll give you a note from your doctor to show the staff at school."

Wendy called over to Sarah, who was walking off to her room, and said "Sarah, you two have that history quiz tomorrow, so show your brother the study materials for that please, and watch out for him tomorrow, dear."

Sarah looked over her shoulder and said "Yes mom." Then she called over, "Come on brother, I have to study also, so get over here."

After that, the evening and night were a bit strained, but not in any unusual way, as a pair of teenage twins being made to work together tended to get.

# CHAPTER TWO:
# THE END OF NORMAL

To Beth Summers, it was a normal day. Keeping tabs on the Hope family twins was looking to be as non-informative as it ever was. And the brother Jon was rumored to be near death after some stupid boyish stunt. Beth was part of a secret society of magic users, just as her parents and their parents had been. The Hope family was descended from a form jumper, an almost mythical and highly terrifying being that almost no real info existed about. They were the kinds of things that were said to be able to raise the dead and throw fireballs around, not no mention being immortal because they possessed unwilling hosts. There were many horror stories, but also no concrete proof that they truly existed. They seemed more like the evil wizards from some over-the-top fantasy game. But there was no denying that almost everyone that seemed to get anywhere researching the form jumpers ended up dead or missing very soon after.

So if they did use magic, it was nothing like the fortune telling magic she used; the only magic she was sure existed that humans had was basic warding and exorcism, plus what could easily be seen as very good sleight of hand or fortune telling. Some folks could do those with real power, but there were a lot more folks that believed they could or pretended they could.

And so as she walked up the hill to school, she saw Sarah Hope and a boy that walked so confidently that she believed Sarah found a boyfriend, until she saw how similar their faces were and realized it was Jonathan Hope.

As she ran over to Sarah, she saw Jonathan mouth the words *fortune teller* to himself, but the only places Beth had ever read fortunes besides at home was the girls' locker room in secret. So she chose to believe she was mistaken, and called over to the Hope twins, "Hey Sarah, how is that dufus up and moving again?" The Hope twins stopped and Sarah's grin and Jon's cold gaze were like night and day. It was no secret Beth and Jonathan were not friends, but he tended to take things a lot more in stride than that.

As Beth got up to the twins and they begin to walk up the hill side-by-side with Sarah in the middle by old habit, Jonathan spoke up and said, "I can walk now. Been that way for a week or so. Any reason I should not be stretching my legs?" He was grinning but his eyes still had a bit of that cold fire from right after Beth's greeting.

Sarah jabbed Jon in the ribs with her elbow and added to Beth's quizzical and  slightly worried face, "He is

14

right about that, although he could be more like himself. Must have hit his head too hard."

At that prompting, Jon laughed and his face was pure innocence as he pointed to his head and joked, "Yeah, that fall must have scrambled the eggs," then he grinned and added, "I'm told I got lucky."

Both girls stared at each other. The Jonathan they knew was a withdrawn unpopular hyperactive boy, with at best one friend in the whole school, a friend that had been acting a bit odd as well.

Then almost as if summoned, the voices of two boys were heard shouting "Hey Gray Area, get back here," as the only friend Jonathan had ran up to Sarah panting, but then looked at Jonathan very strangely.

Jonathan's friend's real name was Aria Gray, a girl that was in the same dance class as Sarah and Beth, and easily the most boyish girl in the whole school.

Jonathan said "Graya?" as he made a fist at his side.

Sarah said "Lover's spat?" as she tried to grin, but looking concerned.

Jonathan then said quickly "Oh right, the doctor's note, see you all in class," as he ran off into the school.

Sarah sighed and looked at Aria as the three girls walked into the school and down the buzzing school hallway on the way to their classroom. "That's some pet name, Aria," she whispered.

Aria looked up and said, "It's a long story. So Jon seems off today."

Beth, still trying to wrap her head around all of this, pointed out, "Well you have been a bit off yourself ever since I bumped into you on the stairway that night."

Aria, the one that had caused Beth to fall by stopping suddenly on a stairway late one night a week before, apologized again, saying "Look, I am really sorry. Tell you what, I'll get you whatever soda you want from the vending machine at lunch."

As they walked into their classroom and at sat at their desks, Beth shook her head and said half jokingly, "Too many calories. I, for one, want to keep my womanly figure."

The three of them laughed at that, then Sarah said, "Hey, you two hear about the two bodies they found on the hill outside town, the ones that were missing persons for ten years?"

Beth sighed. "Isn't there some urban legend about that, a pair of people disappearing close by each other on the same date and time, then showing up many years later dead with all kinds of odd wounds and burns?" She was referencing one of the better known possibly form jumper related conspiracy theories.

Aria, who had been looking more and more thoughtful and a bit concerned, then made an odd request. "Beth, Sarah, I need you both to meet me in the computer classroom half an hour after school ends and not a second sooner. Sarah, bring your brother. Drag him if you must."

The two other girls looked at each other, but heard the seriousness in Aria's tone loud and clear.

Aria added, "If either of you want to know what's going on, then this may be the only chance you get."

Then class abruptly started as Jon took his seat at the far back of the class, but looking interested for once.

Nothing else real odd happened for the rest of the day save Jon being called out by the teacher for answering one of the history quiz questions that asked *what do you think of Jules Caser*, to which Jon had written, *he was a pain in the ass.*

After class ended, Sarah and Beth told Jon about Aria's request, and they all decided they could not pass this up, so they got to the computer class room exactly on time and walked in. Aria was standing, arms folded, looking at the floor, where there was an intricate design drawn within a circle with chalk, and what looked like a slightly grotesque stuffed animal standing in the center of it.

Jon said coolly, "Really Graya, summoning here. Although good place to ambush me."

Aria's tan body looked up, her green eyes cold, short blond hair pulled back into a sharp pony tail she had never worn before, and said "Corewayin, you are planning to stay around and gather your strength, if I am not mistaken.

These two will be in danger as we live in these forms as children, so we owe them some explaining."

Corewayin nodded with Jonathan's body and said, "Looks like you had the same plan, and I am sure our last two bodies have been found by now. Ok but any questions these two have, we should try to answer." Then he pointed at the shape standing on the floor in the chalk circle and asked, "So what's with the gremlin?"

Beth and Sarah both jumped as the thing they had believed to be a malformed stuffed animal looked up with its glowing yellow eyes. Its light blue flesh bumpy and slick looking, it asked in a voice like a hissing tea kettle, "Supposedly to prove a point," it grinned, white fangs gleaming, and added "or to look nice."

Sarah almost fainted. Beth said in a wavering voice "What are you two, really?" not even bothering to adjust her long black hair that Sarah was now partly slumped on, being kept up as much by Beth's shoulder as her own feet. Beth's dark brown eyes studied the two bodies that two of her long term acquaintances had once occupied. Her pale skin seemed flushed.

The one Jon's body had called Graya answered, saying "Form jumpers. Our last bodies died about a week ago; our new ones are a bit young."

Sarah asked weakly, "Where did you come from?" still very confused but seeing how serious and tense everyone else was. She saw that even though she did not understand whatever was happening, it was for real.

Jon's body, that one that had been called Corewayin, answered calmly, "About three thousand years ago and quite a few hundred bodies ago."

Beth murmured, "First line, then."

The one called Graya shook her head and said, "Third line. Both of us were from the time of what is called Ancient Rome. As far as we know, there are three jumpers in the first line. They were from around the time humans first stared farming or maybe writing on clay. Not that I have ever been able to ask them. The one we met was very clever."

Sarah then yelled, "So why are you here? Where is my bother?"

Graya sighed using Aria's face and assured calmly, "Well in the last fight, I killed Corewayin first, then died soon after."

Corewayin added, "Sarah, if I had not taken his body, your bother would have at best been bedridden and incoherent. I am sorry, however, but form jumpers do not pick our new bodies. If it's in range, we may show up after death."

At that Sarah really fainted; her brother's face not being her twin was too much of a shock. Beth held on to her, fear clear in her eyes.

Graya nodded and the gremlin flowed into a nearby computer. To Beth's quizzical face Graya said, "I created that, but as a deal for its good behavior I let it go.

19

Gremlins may be mischievous but they are rarely deadly. Also, I do not know who you are getting your info for, fortune teller, but know that form jumpers attack monsters more then they create them, so we are the best chance you have at surviving if you stay close, but if you make trouble for us, you will pay."

Corewayin added with a wink, "Graya can be a bit uppity sometimes, but remember to use the names of the bodies we have around others." Then he said with a wide grin, "Still a three thousand year lover's spat; well stranger things have happened." He winked again, adding "True story," as he created a small flame on his finger from thin air.

After that the trip home was a blur. Beth was way too shocked and bent out of shape to do much more then walk home after that. The thing Jon was now easily carried Sarah on his back all the way home, and Aria went to the Gray family home.

Beth knew the report tonight to the monster watchers foundation would be a long one with way too many questions she would be required to go and learn the answers to. But more than that, she was not feeling up to seeing whatever Aria and Jon's bodies were now.

# CHAPTER THREE:
# BLOOD DRIVE

The next day Graya, still in the guise of Aria Gray, took the town bus to school just as she had started to do, using the allowance money from her new adoptive family (although as far as they knew, nothing had changed, but how grown up she seemed). Right as she got off the bus she saw Corewayin's new body standing at the bus stop with the nosey young lady Beth Summers sitting down on the bus stop bench, and looking both worried and very uncomfortable.

Graya said in an innocent inquisitive way but with an icy gaze, "Why do you two look so bummed, oh and where's Sarah?"

The eyes of Jonathan Hope blazed with Corewayin's soul, Graya got into a fighting crouch, the other students walked by snickering at how weird the ones they knew as Jonathan and Aria were being.

Beth spoke up with all the strength she could muster. "Because of you two she ran away, so the three of us are going to look for her now."

Aria's face looked at Jonathan and asked "Is that right?" He nodded, so Graya went on and said calmly, "Damn. Well that was faster than I expected."

Corewayin grimaced as Jonathan's voice pointed out "Well you were always the clever one."

Beth stood up and tied to smack both of them in the face, but all of a sudden they were behind her, as if they hadn't even moved at all. *So much for my judo lessons, but I am required to watch those two, whatever they are now*, she thought to herself.

Then Graya took out a cell phone from her pocket as if nothing had happened, and dialed a number as she walked down the roadway from the school and motioned for Beth and Jonathan/Corewayin to come with her. Graya put her current body's phone on speaker and said "Bert, I know you are there, I need to find one of those mage blooded girls from yesterday, the one without any magic abilities."

The gremlin Graya had summoned the day before replied over the phone "Already? Ok, I have access to enough of the human's satellites to mange that. Hold on... ok there's an old civil war graveyard on a small hill in some woods around five miles away. Just remember that a necromancer once lived around there."

Graya grinned and said "And any other info will cost me, ok thanks" with that she turned off the phone.

Corewayin asked, "So which civil war did that elder breed mean?"

Graya sighed and said "Corewayin, you really have to learn how to keep all the wars you have been in straight."

Corewayin smiled. Beth still found Jonathan's face saying what it did now spooky, but she could see a strength and sadness there as well, one very at odds with how inhuman Jonathan was supposed to be.

Graya grumbled "Ok, enough dilly dallying, I'll bring the girl with me. Corewayin or whatever you want to be called, now follow me." With that, Aria's body hoisted Beth up one-handed over one shoulder like a half-full bag of apples, and then to Beth's utter disbelief a sheet of ice formed under Aria's feet, and they were off like a motorcycle.

Beth half turned to see Jonathan's body sliding after them on a sheet of dirt. To try to take her mind off of all the weirdness she asked Corewayin, who was now moving along next to Graya, "Could one of you explain more of this to me?"

Corewayin grinned and said, "And here I thought Benjamin Franklin or the general Hannibal asked too many questions! My thing is fire and earth magic. I am also rather skilled with weapons and a skilled enchanter. Aria, or rather Graya over there uses water and lighting magic mostly, but ice spells, and steam magic plus summoning and controlling monsters on purpose are well within her power. Anything else will have to wait."

Aria's face was glaring at Corewayin by now as she said "I know this girl will not leave us alone until she knows everything about us, or that knowledge kills her, but come on, at least make her work for it." The lonely twist to Aria's mouth seemed to be something only Beth was aware of.

Then they arrived at a small overgrown hill with a low crumbing wall and many heavily weathered gravestones, plus one lonely stone monument in the center of it all.

Jonathan turned to look at Beth, his gaze and stance as completely unfamiliar to Beth as they were his current body, then in a tone used to command, the thing that Jonathan had become requested, "This will get a bit hairy, Beth. A minor magic user would die if unarmed here, so please endeavor to stay out of our way."

Graya, now not even trying to behave like Aria, or any teenage high school tomboy Beth had ever known at all, asked, "You felt that too? Looks that one of the necromancer's pets is still active."

Corewayin nodded. "Feral vampire, only thing it could be."

Graya sighed, disappointed. "Damn. Not even a true monster. At least it is a high grade reanimated beast."

A new voice chimed in from behind the only tall monument in the middle of the small overgrown graveyard. "Yes, well you are right about that, magic and blood are my fuel, and just when I was thinking I'd have to live on only blood, four magic users show, two of them almost as strong as my late master."

At that, a shadowy form, like a hunched over hairless wolf, with pure white skin, covered in old rags, leapt out from behind the monument at Beth in such a blur that she had just enough time to cower a few steps behind Graya and Corewayin.

Then almost as the beast's long clawed hands were going to grab her throat, the vampire's long inhuman face and blood-red eyes filled with the thrill of the hunt, a shovel covered in fire bisected the vampire neatly in half.

Graya sighed again and repeated "Not even a true monster," as the last of the vampire burned away in a cool bluish purple flame. Corewayin brought the old once-discarded shovel he had just picked up that was still covered in fire to rest headfirst at his feet.

Then to Beth's terrified face he commented, "Ok, you look for our friend here, I'll stand guard." Then to Graya he asked, "So Aria, you sure that troublesome descendant of mine is here?"

Graya looked shocked for a second, then replied "Right, I thought the name Hope was familiar," then she smiled and said "Yeah I am sure, but we would totally freak her out if we just came to pick her up."

Soon after, Beth found Sarah, who was slumped at the base of the monument, and seemingly asleep. Just as

Beth was trying to think if she could get Sarah away from the monsters that now inhabited her classmates, Corewayin's voice called over. "Looks all clear. I'll be playing hooky today, but if Sarah could stay over at your place tonight, that may be good."

Then after half a minute later, with no sounds after that remark, Beth looked around the side of the monument. The only thing out of place was a shovel stuck in the ground and a few wispy rags draped over it like a limp scarecrow.

A bit later, with Beth still holding her friend, Sarah's eyes opened with a start as she desperately tried to escape Beth's loose grasp. Beth let go and watched Sarah with every sign of pity until her old friend slumped down on the ground and asked while looking around, "Where am I?"

Beth shot back in a worried tone "What's the last thing you remember? I am here for you."

Sarah closed her eyes tight, then said "I packed a bag last night, slipped out a window and ran. Someone was following me, so I tried to lose them in the woods. Then you were here. That's it. What time is it? What happened to me this time?" Sarah proceeded to cry into her hands.

Beth stated firmly, "Well, the school day started a bit ago, and I dragged the two..." She paused, looking for the right words "...things, with me looking for you. Something they called a vampire had you, hence the scenery, and well, Corewayin killed it."

At the name Corewayin, Sarah started to sob more.

"That thing took my brother. I can't go back, not yet, not today, not..." she stopped mid-sentence and looked at Beth as she asked in tears, then added, "Help me."

Beth nodded and offered, "Well how about you come to my home? I may be able to help you get answers about this. We will say you fainted and are going be sleeping over at my place to study."

Sarah nodded and smiled a little, then said meekly, "Ok," but with more strength than before.

# CHAPTER FOUR:
# SHARDS OF PEACE

That night Sarah stayed over the Summers residence. Cindy Summers, Beth's mom, was a bit surprised when Beth and Sarah shuffled through the door, drained a few hours after the school day had started. Before Cindy could speak up, Beth held out a hand and said "A lot happened. I invited Sarah so stay the night. She is a bit in shock, please see to her. I have to make my report to the foundation now."

Cindy could see no sign that Beth was joking. Unscheduled reports were only for very big and important sudden discoveries, but one look at the two girls in front of her and Beth's mom could tell this was one of those times. Although just what the monster watchers foundation would tell her was likely not very much. Form jumper research was often avoided and complete reliable firsthand info was nonexistent, not because it was a taboo, but because such research had claimed so many lives that form jumpers were more an urban legend often linked to unexplained and odd events. For that reason it was used to break in young members of the secret society the Summers family belonged to, because the chances of any real info being found was almost as low as the survival rate of those rumored to have found anything real.

Cindy took Sarah by the hand and led her into the kitchen, with one last look behind her shoulder at her now grim-faced daughter. Cindy got Sarah to help cook lunch, then two hours later Beth showed up.

Sarah looked up and said "So how did it go?" That was longest string of words she had uttered for most of the day.

Beth scratched her head, then stretched and after a huge yawn she said, "Too many damn follow-up questions. I am going to have to ask Corewayin..." She paused and looked at Sarah who was stuffing her face, and not cringing near as much as Beth was after saying the name of the thing inhabiting her friend's twin brother. Beth finished slowly "...a lot of stuff tomorrow."

Sarah sighed and said, after swallowing a large bite of the lasagna she had been working on, "Just write them down and hand those two fools a list. I am sure one of them would answer them, if just to humor us."

Beth nodded. "Yeah, like it or not, they seem to be going out of their way to be helpful. I am still not sure why."

Cindy finally spoke up and stated "Beth honey, it is not good to discuss the foundation's business with anyone but the masters."

Beth pointed at Sarah's now slack apologetic face and said "Sarah Hope, repeat nothing you hear today," then looking at Cindy Summers she added, "Mom, believe it or not, my buddy here has higher clearance for this info then you do, because she is the key to getting the two form jumpers that keep following us around to open up."

Cindy looked dubious and asked, "Are you sure? Old names aside, really two of them? How are you alive?"

Sarah spoke up and said "Because last time they defended us."

Beth added, "From a vampire as if it was thin air. Anyway Sarah, how do you feel?"

Sarah Hope stared at the ceiling above the table they were sitting at and pointed out "I do not think they mean any of us harm, and well, it's not like I can run away, regardless of what my brother is now."

After that Sarah and Beth sat watching the news until night time, after Cindy and Sarah had called the Hope family and told Sarah's folks that she wanted to get Beth to help her study. Sarah curled up in a sleeping bag. Cindy Summers stopped her daughter as Beth was just finishing up brushing her teeth and said "Be careful, hon."

Beth looked up and said in a determined voice, "Of course I will be."

Cindy looked at her daughter's stubborn but calm face for a time, then asked "You know, Corewayin is supposed to be the name of the form jumper the Hope family is descended from."

Beth nodded and said, "One of many things I need to know."

And with that, the two girls slept more soundly then they had in a long time due to how exhausting their day had been.

The next day Beth slipped the list of questions the masters of the monster watchers foundation had asked into Jonathan Hope's hand, for the 3000 year old thing Corewayin to answer.

Other than that, and Bert the gremlin disguised in human form teaching the computer class, nothing too odd happened.

Before Aria, Beth, Sarah and Jon went home after school (Sarah with Jon, to his surprise and that of the two others), Jon got the four of them together at the town bus stop in front of school and said, "All three of you need to show up at the Hope family house before school tomorrow. I have something helpful to give each of you."

That night Corewayin did not go to sleep. He stayed up all night in the garage to finish what he told his current body's parents was a last minute show-and-tell project he had to elaborate on. It seemed he had done the same thing the night before when Sarah was at Beth's home finding herself.

The next morning Aria and Beth came over early. If they had shown up a few minutes before, they would have been getting Sarah out of bed. As the three girls entered the Hope family garage, Jon Hope's face peeked up from behind a stack of tires and he called over, "Just in time."

"What is this about, Corewayin?" the three girls said in unison, then stared at each other.

Corewayin grumbled. "Just do not get too used to that. It's Jon to anyone else I know."

Then he handed Beth a case of darts, Sarah a large knife. Graya ended up holding a telescoping baton in Aria Gray's hands, and lastly Corewayin look out an ice pick.

Graya smiled and said, "This is very nice work, Jon." She smiled as she used Corewayin's body's name, ignoring Sarah's glare.

Beth asked, "So what's the point of this?"

Graya looked at Corewayin and said "Seeing auras looks like a dead art as well."

Corewayin explained. "I enchanted these with magic, so they should be very effective against monsters, far more then a non-enchanted version." Then he looked at Beth, saying "That case is a bit different than the other items, Beth. In short, focus some magic into it when it has darts in it and the darts will be enchanted for about a day when taken out of the case. Also, the list of questions you handed me should be in there as well."

Beth said, "I have no idea how to focus power like that."

Graya sighed, saying "You both could be monster hunters, you both absorb magic given off by others. Kill enough monsters and you may be able to have limited use of true magic."

Beth was shocked and said "So we would become form jumpers? I have never heard of something happening like that."

Corewayin said firmly to Sarah and Beth's terrified faces, "Because that's not possible. Form jumpers were made by mortal true magic users when such things still existed, and all of them died in the Titan Wars."

Graya looked worried and distant as she recalled old events, then shook her head and added "The only time form jumpers died en masse was against those things. There are about four left of them. They were the only monsters to exist before the form jumpers."

Sarah asked, "You can die?"

Corewayin said, "Only if there is no mortal human body of the same gender in range, but whether we truly die or not is unclear."

After that, Beth and Graya put the weapons Corewayin had given them in their school bags. Sarah hid the enchanted knife she had been given in her room, and Corewayin put his new weapon in a bag of camping supplies the last resident of his body had owned. After that, the four of them went to school.

As it was early, the four of them slowly walked the mile and a half. On the way, Sarah asked Corewayin, "So Jon, you may not recall this, but us three" she indicated Beth and Aria/Graya, "have dance class after school, so I'll see you later."

Aria's body shrugged as Graya said, "Well why not? Got to stay in shape." Then she grinned. "Plus I am learning some things for once."

Jon's face grinned widely and informed his three companions, "Well, I have signed up for the archery club, so I'll see you three right after dance lets out." Then to the three dubious looks he was getting Corewayin added, "The classes get out at the same time, it's just been a while since I really used a bow."

Sarah could not help it and asked "Like when?"

Corewayin thought for a little bit and said "Maybe the battle of Hastings, or all the wars in the 100 Years War." He still was thinking deeply a few minutes later, then corrected himself as Beth and Sarah both jumped, surprised after Corewayin started talking again. "No, it was during the industrial revolution in Siberia."

Graya shook her head and chided. "Look Jon." She said the name Jon slowly as if talking to a child. "I keep telling you keep all those wars straight."

About half way to the school, as the four of them walked along the sidewalk near the small town's tree lined main road, Beth asked, "So did either of you fight a Titan?"

Graya all of a sudden looked distant and uncomfortable for once, as Corewayin said, "Yes, both of us were in a few mass battles against those. It's about the only thing we fear." Then after shooting a worried look at Graya he went on. "We will give you one example and only one. In a battle I was in near Athens a little after the Roman Empire took over fifty form jumpers and twenty thousand ancient Roman heavy infantrymen fought one Titan, I was the only one that survived still in a body. A few of the other form jumper's minds still wander that area to this day. Needless to say, the Titan was very amused as it left the field of battle."

Beth and Sarah both looked from Corewayin to Graya almost speechless. As Beth opened her mouth to ask a follow-up question, Sarah put her hand on Beth's shoulder, shaking her head as she pointed out, "Everyone has their secrets, let's just leave it at this for now." Graya then looked relived and nodded her thanks to Sarah.

At computer class later that day Bert the Gremlin, still masquerading as Bert the new computer teacher, called Graya into the hallway by saying, "We need to have a chat about your grades, Miss Gray." In the hallway Bert said "That necromancer from before may still be around. It's possible he is the biology teacher."

Graya asked, "Does he also teach archery?"

Bert answered, "Yes, why?"

Graya smiled. "Because I am sure someone else is already looking into it," as she thought *so Corewayin, you can plan ahead, but if not, this should be interesting either way.*

# CHAPTER FIVE:
# BURNING DESIRE

After school and the classes, Jon was leaning against the bus stop notice board when Beth, Sarah and Aria Gray were walking down the small hill that led from their school building. Without a word, the four classmates walked down in the direction of their neighborhoods, as the four of them lived within a couple of streets of one another. They tended to use the same town bus, but got on at different stops.

As they were passing a small grassy field, Graya stopped and said loudly and menacingly, "I can sense all of you, so stop hiding."

Her three companions also stopped as Corewayin put Jon's body between the field and his two mortal companions. A few seconds later something that looked like a man stepped out from behind a tree. Corewayin told the two girls he was guarding, "Both of you, do not fight these things, stay behind me and Aria."

The late middle-aged man stepped forward. He had balding gray brown hair, flushed skin and dark brown eyes that had a disquieting fire to them; at least that was what it looked like to Sarah and Beth.

Graya said, "Jon, think you can let the two others absorb most of the power from these?" As she made a quick flick of her wrist, hands still at her side but tense, a globe of water appeared around the man's head, then the water was swiftly engulfed in turn by electricity, causing the man's head to explode but his body to melt into a blob of still moving magma, as four other such things burst from the tree line.

Sarah gaped and said, "What the hell are those things?" Beth threw an enchanted dart at one of the smaller blobs. The dart was swiftly melted and absorbed by the blob, as it seemed to swell a bit.

Three of the blobs then started to make a bee line for Beth as Corewayin yelled "Idiot, these are fire elementals, a whole family of them, stay back! They are at worst third generation."

At that, a circular wall of clay that Corewayin had summoned surrounded Beth and Sarah. Then he directed a look of resolve and a grin at Graya's determined and focused face. Graya, for her part, was keeping track of Corewayin in her peripheral vision and sensing his aura of magic power, but otherwise was purely focusing on the attackers around them.

Corewayin got into an old hand-to-hand / magic casting combat stance with an ease of long use, and smothered two of the attackers under a pile of dirt. Graya then swept those two and one other away with a burst of water summoned from the water vapor in the air around them. After, Corewayin encased and crushed the last two in a prison of rock called from the ground under their attackers' burning blobby bodies.

At that, the wall around Beth and Sarah crumbled, and the two mortal girls looked around at their two saviors putting the area back to how it was (so more or less a few cracks and odd piles of dust were all that remained of the fight). Sarah asked in a voice that was very calm, due in large part because by now she was used to and expecting all kinds of weirdness, "So at a guess, are we being targeted or tested?"

Corewayin looked up and with a wide grin that was the same as the first occupant of his body once made said, "Maybe a little of both, although the more magic you have, the tastier you look to the monsters."

Beth raised an eyebrow and inquired, "Then why make them?"

Graya, now back to playing the part of Aria for the most part, pointed out "How about we get moving? This was likely a probing attack by something more powerful."

Then as they started to walk back to their homes, Aria/Graya asked, "Beth, any chance I could stay at your place tonight after I look into a few things?"

Beth after a short pause agreed. "Yeah sure, but why....?"

Corewayin said in a tone very much like Jon, "Strength in numbers. Like it or not, you two are more vulnerable than a fifth generation form jumper." Then to Graya he added, "Aria, I'll look after these two at Beth's place until you are back, then sis and I will go back home for tonight."

Then after realizing Corewayin was talking a lot like Jon, the former resident of his body, Graya pointed out right before running off, "Form jumpers keep many of the memories of the bodies they show up in. That can make their identity a bit blurred, for the lucky ones," then she ran off, shouting "See ya later!"

After that Beth, Corewayin, and Sarah walked to Beth's home in silence. After a time Sarah grumbled angrily to herself. "And just when I was getting good at dealing with this."

Corewayin grunted. "You think that's hard. The pain of dying in battle is simple. Getting attached to mortals that often do not even recognize you, that's hard. Beatrice Hope, for example."

Sarah started. "What does one of my old ancestors have to do..." Then after a few seconds of silence she said, "Wait, you are also one of my ancestors?"

Corewayin nodded. His current face, Sarah's twin's face, had a grim look, with eyes showing regret deep enough to drown in. He said "I can't pick what body I go to, and this one would have died without me, but I still regret taking over this boy's body and causing my own blood to suffer. That the ancestor you speak of was a man whose body I took over at least 200 years ago does not diminish that."

As they were arriving at Beth's home, three fire trucks sped by, as billowing smoke hovered over the tree tops from a few streets away. Soon after, as the three companions sat on the front patio in silence of Beth's family residence, Beth's mom Cindy made them lemonade, and after hearing a bit about the attack, had agreed to let Aria stay the night as long as she provided any clarifying info Beth may need to fulfill her nightly report to the monster watchers foundation, to which Aria later agreed, so long as the info was directly related to the events of the day.

A short while later Graya showed up. Corewayin nodded over the smoke plume that was still expanding from the direction she had come from. Graya nodded and said, "Had to cover their trail," then for the others' benefit, she elaborated. "The elementals were masquerading as a husband, wife and three kids. The oldest was third generation and 200 or so years old, the youngest 16 years old, so no elder breeds, just lesser versions of some others that were made by one older, more powerful elemental. Same signature as that vampire, however.

Corewayin then said, "The aura seems a lot like Stone's work." Graya nodded as Corewayin explained, "First generation form jumper."

Beth asked, "What's the difference?"

Graya said, "Five generations or lines of power. The older ones are more powerful. The first ones were made by the Titans and a few mortal true magic users. All others were made by the now extinct mortal true magic users from other true magic users, except for the fifth line. They were made from minor magic users by form jumpers after the Titan Wars but before the current all-time low in the planet's natural magic."

Corewayin explained to the very confused but interested looks he and Graya were getting, "First generation form jumpers each have five types of powers, including very high level ones that, like necromancy, are stupidly simple for them, but extremely hard trial-and-error-affairs for anyone else. Plus their bodies do not age, and when they die they go to another body. Their vitality and magic, however, are one and the same. Other than that, second line are like myself but have three magic powers. Graya and I each have two. We are third line. Fourth line have one. They are basically monster hunters with a ton of natural magic that shift bodies like I do. Then fifth line have minor powers: fortune telling, warding and so on; but most fifth lines that live in a body long enough awaken a true magic power which they lose upon death, and must regain over time in any new body. There have been 20,000 or so form jumpers all told, but nowadays after the Titan Wars, we are down to 5,000 or so active ones. The others are likely floating around somewhere, just not walking in a body."

After that, Sarah and Corewayin went back to the Hope family home, both wishing the last day of school that week would not be so completely nuts.

That night, as Beth Summers and Aria Gray/Graya were putting out two sleeping bags that Cindy Summers had been able to scrounge up from the her family's attic, Beth asked, "Graya, you and Corewayin have known each other a long time, right? I get the feeling you two were not always such bitter rivals. What changed?"

Aria's face suddenly looked more weary and tired then anyone in a sixteen-year-old's body had any right to look. Put simply, her expression looked like it would belong on a very old woman looking back at a past deep regret. She answered in a soft voice, more to herself than to Beth, "I suppose you have that right." Then she looked up at Beth in a calm but distant way, completely at odds with the Aria Gray her body had once entirely been.

Beth thought to herself, *wow, maybe this old, wizened side is more or less the real Graya*, and it scared Beth to realize just how different this was from what Aria's body had once been, before Graya took it.

Graya just continued, seemingly oblivious to everything. "Back when Corewayin and I were still in the bodies were had been born in, Corewayin was under command of Julius Caesar, before Caesar was emperor of Rome, on an expedition into what is now England. My tribe got a bit too close for comfort. We were almost all killed. Corewayin was able to get some of the tribe spared, myself included, at our last camp. The young female true magic users were seen as very useful. Corewayin later took me as his wife. I was a very useful slave before he purchased me and freed me. We died of old age, but both came back. We found each other in our new bodies, argued, had an on/off love affair, had a son who was later possessed by Stone. We call him Stone as that's all we could pronounce from his first name, some ancient Bronze Age language from before humans could write. Anyway, we had a falling out. After that, Corewayin fought in so many wars because that's all he really knew and he could not die. I studied and found other form jumpers, and we have been in a cycle of grief and war with each other and the world ever since, but have always found each other and stayed nearby."

Beth was flabbergasted and all she could sputter was, "So you two are in love or something?"

Graya shrugged and said calmly, now back to the tomboyish devil-may-care persona Aria had often displayed, "I really do not know. We have killed and hunted each other through so many lifetimes. If we both could come to terms with that pain and forgive it, then maybe someday, but for now we live for the bodies we took over. I know Corewayin and myself feel bad about taking over these forms we have now; reminds us of the past too much." She shrugged again sadly and added, "Well probably."

# CHAPTER SIX:
# FROZEN HOPE. COOL RESOLVE.

Late that night, the Summer family home phone went off. Beth groggily picked it up. Corewayin was on the other end and with Jon Hope's voice he almost shouted "I do not have long, just get yourself and Graya on the move now! Some fool sent an elder breed ice giant after us. Sarah and I are going to try to run for it. Oh crap!" The line went dead. The shattering, bellowing, and screaming from the background over the phone was not a good sign either.

As Beth put the phone down slowly and turned around, she almost bumped into Graya, who was standing behind her. Before Beth could say anything, Graya simply said, "Yeah, I heard, I'll go and try to help out. Stone must really want us dead, and after all this time, too."

Beth nodded and said, "I'll go too." She could see Graya's very upset and conflicted look on Aria's face, so Beth clarified, "I need to make sure Sarah is ok."

Graya nodded, looking a bit relieved, and said sternly, "Ok, but keep it at that; do nothing to get yourself killed."

After they both bundled up and Beth left a note for her mother, they ran onward toward the Hope family home a few blocks away, weapons in hand, anger in their hearts, and concern in their minds.

Neither was prepared for what they found. Besides the splintered mailbox, the rest of what had been the Hope family home was demolished to the ground and frozen solid. Two pair of human footprints led off from where the ice was little by little giving way to a frozen muck. In the same direction were a pair of giant prints that were filling with slush. Without a second thought, and after a few swift glances at the home turned frozen crater, Beth and Graya hurried off after the footprints of what was left of the Hope family, booming footfalls in the distance no doubt also on their tail.

In the woods, near a small now very frozen lake, Corewayin/Jon Hope and Sarah Hope stared frozen death in the face: the giant that had leveled the Hope family home along with Jeff and Wendy Hope. Corewayin could see Sarah was in a killing mood, the enchanted knife he had given her held in two white knuckled hands. *There is no stopping her from being rash. Damn, I can't let her die too, I have far too many regrets even for an almost immortal like myself,* Corewayin grudgingly realized, so he called to Sarah who was standing at his back, knife still out. "Sarah, back me up, or run for it. I would prefer if you stay safe at least."

Sarah spat, "Shut up monster, you may look like my brother, and be some long-dead ancestor of my family, but do not think that gives you the right to tell me how to live, after all that's happened!"

A voice called out near them from the tree line as Graya and Beth rushed over, Graya shouting, "Then kill him after if you can. I'm sure the giant is out for all of our blood, so blood feuds any time but now, ok?"

As they were talking, the giant rumbled out of the lake it had fallen in, that had frozen solid soon after.

As it walked toward them, plants and grass ensnared its feet just as Graya electrified the water it was walking out of. Sarah looked at Beth as she commanded the plants around them for the first time. Corewayin then called over to Sarah, "Oh enraged descendent, do me a favor. Try to use true magic before you try to kick any monster's ass. Most have quite the temper."

Graya called over, "I'll agree with the meathead on this one. Rage has no place on the battlefield unless you truly have a death wish."

Corewayin added, "So if you want to kill me, Sarah, you have to be alive, but then my mind will be on its way again, and I'd prefer if I did not have to take over another body so soon," as he dodged a huge block of ice that had once been a tree which plowed into the ground he had been standing on.

A tree branch then fell on the ice giant's head, courtesy of Beth, as three darts hit one of its huge ice-blue eyes.

Graya slammed the baton Corewayin had enchanted for her into the giant's left calf. Its light blue flesh spasmed with the electricity Graya poured in through her baton. The giant then made a grab for Sarah as she tried to edge closer to stab something. As the giant's fist was folding around her, a huge flash of light burst around her, making the giant clutch at its remaining good eye. One massive fireball to its white whiskered face later, and the giant was toast, or least burned to a nice smoking cinder that transformed into a mound of cool bluish ash picked up by the wind.

Sarah was staring at her hands as she mumbled, "What the hell was that?"

Graya patted Sarah on the back and said triumphantly, "You are a monster hunter!" Then to Sarah's terrified gaze and bewildered look, Graya added, "Still human and mortal, but with some limited magic, light control by the looks of it."

Corewayin nodded and added, "And Beth got plant manipulation, by the looks of it."

Then as he was staring off into space after the dissipating ash he added, "Also, the only way to kill a form jumper totally would be to make it so their essence, or whatever transferred themselves from body to body, could be found and destroyed. As long as there is a body to go to, I can't die."

Sarah said angrily, "Well you should. My parents and brother died because of you."

Corewayin looked her straight in the eyes and said, "I would like nothing more than to die. I have lived through more than enough pain. Being used to it does not make it right."

Beth then spoke up. "How about we find and beat the snot out of whoever has been hunting us, then work out whose fault things are and what will be done about it?"

Graya looked at Sarah and said, "We know what you are going through, but unless we find Stone, we still are going to be hunted."

Corewayin nodded, then said, "He is a form jumper, but Graya and I owe him some pain, for the same reason you are mad at me, Sarah. After that, if this body still lives, I'll leave its fate up to you."

Sarah replied sternly, "Well, we'd better get to work then. The sooner the better."

Corewayin instructed, "I say we stake out the school. I am almost positive the form jumper we are after is the biology teacher Raymond Green. His aura and those of the monsters that have attacked us are very similar, the vampire included."

Graya laughed as she said, "Well, you still surprise me sometimes, meathead."

Sarah and Beth just looked at each other. Beth shrugged and Sarah nodded. Sarah stated what they both were thinking. "Ok, what have we got to lose?"

Corewayin grimaced and said, "Your lives, perhaps?"

Sarah slapped his face as he continued unfazed. "If Raymond is Stone the first generation form jumper, then fighting him is out of the league of any mortals." Then he added as he patted Sarah's head and looked calmly into her eyes, despite the glare he was getting from her and Graya, although for fairly different reasons, "To settle the score with me, you will need to be alive."

After looking on for a few minutes as the looks started to cool almost as much as the frosty air around them, in the small clearing they had fought the frost giant, Beth started to walk toward the school as she shouted behind herself, "Quit flirting and get a move on!" A few frosty glares and flushed cheeks in her direction later, the four of them walked away from the clearing, its frozen state at odds with it being the middle of summer.

# CHAPTER SEVEN:
# THE END OF NORMAL DAYS

When the four teenagers (although to be fair, two of those "teenagers" had around 3,000 years of skills and memories, not to mention the powers and personalities they had been developing) got to the small hill across from the school, a man was waiting for them. He had lightly tanned skin with dark red hair and light brown eyes that were almost red. He was in a white shirt and lab coat with a tie and black pants plus some heavy work boots.

The man smiled at Corewayin, who looked a bit disheveled in his light denim jacket, mud-caked jeans and sneakers, as well as the thin green shirt that now sported a few cuts from all the running and fighting earlier. The stranger said, "Took you long enough. Is biding your time something new, Corewayin?"

Graya snarled "Stone," making it sound more of a curse said through clenched teeth than a word.

Beth took hold of Sarah's arm and pulled her away from the fight halfway up the hill, as the three form jumpers stood at the top. Then it started to rain, as Graya's anger and pain produced a thunderstorm as intense as it was localized right over the small hill.

Stone grinned as he said, "You almost had me. Finding my grandson who had the same aura was very lucky for you, or deadly."

Corewayin snorted as he asked, "So that body's grandson is named Raymond Green? It's creepy how the ones of the first bloodline take over a body, then halt the aging process."

Stone shook his head. "Being stuck as a baby is not that fun."

Graya spat the words, "So what now? Going to gloat how you took over the child Corewayin and I had in our second lives?"

Stone grinned wickedly and pointed out with badly faked surprise, "What, me?" Then he smiled as he added sarcastically, "How many times were you burned at the stake as a witch again, mother?"

Before Graya could fly off the handle and charge madly at the still smirking Stone, a puddle of magma suddenly formed under Stone's feet, courtesy of Corewayin.

Then with an angry shout, Stone leapt back and raised his hand, and a bubble of energy surrounded the three combatants. Stone smiled as he cackled, "I always wanted to test this spell, to see if I could cut off a form jumper from going to a new body and bind them to this place."

Graya rolled her eyes as she glared at the two men before her, and said sarcastically but red-faced, "Of course he planned for this."

Corewayin grinned as he looked encouragingly at Graya. "Well," he pointed out, "let's see if that means we can get rid of him by using this!"

Graya managed to smile, "If we do that, how about trying to coexist peacefully together for the next three lifetimes, meathead?"

Corewayin smiled and said, "Why not? Sounds refreshing, but let's focus on finishing this first," as he dodged a blast of wind Stone had aimed at him.

Graya threw a wide spread of icicles encased in lightning at Stone as Corewayin quickly regained his balance.

Stone then formed the mud around him into a wall of rock, using alchemy and earth magic at the same time.

Then within the barrier of rock Stone had created literally by magic, a volcanic eruption from the puddle of magma Corewayin had called forth around ten seconds before poured lava all around and over him, forcing the now badly burned Stone to use his wind magic to levitate away from it.

This made him a perfect target for a lighting strike, which Graya took full advantage of, calling down three spheres of ball lighting that enshrouded Stone from all sides.

With one huge blast of wind magic throwing dust, ash, and shards of ice all over the impromptu field of battle, Stone hit the ground hard and rolled a few times on the ground. Near death, he held up his hand to the bubble of energy he had used in an attempt to bind the essence of his two old foes.

Graya and Corewayin could see the barrier was falling apart, but Graya, unwilling to let Stone flee, focused her magic into the binding energies around them, trying maintain its function until Stone's body died. Corewayin helped by burning Stone's current form to ash.

Corewayin grunted. "Having one's life force be one and the same as their magic can be powerful, but killing your stolen body's health in a bid to destroy is wasteful."

Graya coughed decisively, as a small shade was formed, trapped in the binding's embrace. "Any last words for our friend here?"

Corewayin nodded. "If there is an afterlife, he can say hi to death for us, and if he meets our son's ghost, then he is in the wrong damn place."

Graya smiled, "Well said." She weaved a complex anti-summoning spell into the binding trap that Stone had placed on the hill to trap and/or toy with them, then with an otherworldly scream five thousand plus years in the making, Stone was gone. A few strands of his mind remained floating around, but were far too shredded to take over anyone unlucky enough to reabsorb Stone's now very shattered soul.

At that, Graya looked up at Corewayin and kissed him on the lips, just as Beth and Sarah were racing up the hill to see what had just yelled in such an unearthly manner.

The sight of Jon and Aria's bodies kissing like long-lost lovers halted the two mortal girls in their tracks. After two minutes of watching Graya/Aria and Jon/Corewayin staring into each other's eyes, Sarah cleared her throat loudly as Beth grinned slightly and commented, "Well, this is awkward, bad time?"

Sarah just shook her head and said, "Even if you had not taken those bodies, those two would have done that at some point."

Graya, now looking very embarrassed with herself and slightly mad at either Corewayin or the world, retorted, "Well, their memories say they did a few times."

Corewayin sighed, "Only because Aria was pushy about getting her first kiss."

Beth barely held in a giggle, more as a favor to Sarah and her now embarrassed and slightly revolted look, than anything else. After quickly composing herself, Beth requested, "I'd like to have the four of us give a report of this to the monster watchers foundation before we start to try to kill each other, if that's how this goes."

Corewayin nodded as Graya calmly spoke for both of them. "Ok I can live with that, but after that, the two of us would like to be on our way." She held up her hands, forestalling any hasty comments from the other girls, her still slightly flushed cheeks showing more then she was saying. Then she finished, "We will keep these bodies as safe as we can and will not destroy them ourselves. We have a truce for the next few lives."

At that, Sarah burst into movement, making five illusionary copies of herself as she and her doubles charged Graya with knife outstretched, as the ash and ice from the last battle kept falling around them like a hail storm on a smoldering house. Suddenly everything on the hill was enveloped in a blinding mist of grit and steam that Graya had created. Sarah and Beth stood there gagging along with Sarah's mirror images.

When the dust settled and steam stopped filling the lungs of the two mortal friends, the only sign of their quarry was a long note burned into the bedrock of the hill. It read:

> *We will meet again. Find us if you can. But if*
> *you can rid our very souls from this earth*
> *someday, then _we_ will find _you_. Catch us if you*
> *can! It will be a bumpy ride one way or another.*

> *p.s. sorry for the pain*

Beth shook her head. "Well, they are not being grandiose," she murmured with equal parts sarcasm and frustration.

Sarah just took Beth's arm and said matter-of-factly, "Come on, we've still got that report to send, plus I have a request. Your bosses owe me, after all."

Beth could see Sarah would demand something from the masters of the monster watchers foundation regardless of how unlikely it was she was to get it.

And so they headed back to the Summers residence, down through the mud, as the thunderstorm Graya's rage had made was picked up by the other clouds and quickly spread across the sky, just as it had done a few weeks before. And so the storm raged as the two friends walked, as they raged and thought to themselves, unwilling to give up, but working out their next steps, raw emotion colliding with deeply held resolve. On the walk home they had taken so many times before, all they had to do now was plan, prepare and wait, as they honed their skills and power, and planned for the next war.

# ABOUT THE AUTHOR

Evan A. Cushing lives in Salem, Massachusetts.

Made in the USA
Middletown, DE
30 August 2022